**For Morgan and Jemima, who are sometimes shy.**
**C. W.**

**To everybody that would like to be a lion, just for one day!**
**F. C.**

First published in Great Britain in 2006 by Gullane Children's Books
This paperback edition published in 2007 by
**Gullane Children's Books**
an imprint of Pinwheel Limited

Winchester House, 259-269 Old Marylebone Road,
London NW1 5XJ

1 3 5 7 9 10 8 6 4 2

Text © Carrie Weston 2006
Illustrations © Francesca Chessa 2006

The right of Carrie Weston and Francesca Chessa to be identified as the author and illustrator of this work
has been asserted by them in accordance with the Copyright, Designs and Patents Act, 1988.
A CIP record for this title is available from the British Library.

ISBN-13: 978-1-86233-656-8
ISBN-10: 1-86233-656-3

Printed and bound in China

# When BRIAN Was A LiON

Carrie Weston ★ Francesca Chessa

GULLANE
CHILDREN'S BOOKS

One morning the postman brought something for Brian.
It was an invitation to a fancy dress party.
Brian frowned. He didn't want to wear
a fancy dress.
"But you can be an astronaut,
or a fire-fighter, or a clown,
or a pirate," said Mum.
"You can be anything!"

"It's a *girls'* party," said Brian.

The next day Mum took Brian shopping for Caitlin's present.
They looked at puzzles, games, books, fairy wands and dolls.
Finally, Mum held up a big, cuddly lion.
"What about this?" she asked.
Brian shrugged.
"I think Caitlin will love it," said Mum.
"And it's given me an idea!"

When they got home Mum started searching.

She found some wool, some holey tights, a pair of mittens,

a few buttons, and an old jumper that Grandma had knitted.

"This will do," she said.

On Saturday morning Brian woke up with a start.
There was something lying on his chair.
He crept out of bed . . .
and tip-toed across the floor . . .
It was a lion costume! Oh no! Caitlin's party!

Brian put the costume on. He looked in the mirror.
He sighed.

"Do you like it?" asked Mum.
"Dressing up is stupid," whined Brian.
"Do I have to go?"
"I promised Caitlin's mum I'd help,"
said Mum. "Besides, I'm sure you'll
enjoy it when you get there."

There were lots of girls at the party.
There was a twirling ballerina, a puffed-up Cinderella,
two Snow Whites and at least five sparkly fairies.

Brian groaned.
Then the dancing started.

The twirling ballerina did a pirouette on Brian's tail.
A sparkly fairy poked him with her wand . . .

. . . and clumsy Cinderella stood
on his paw.

# OUch!

It hurt.

Brian had had enough. He was
getting hot and itchy in his lion suit.
"I don't like this party!" he muttered. He decided to hide
under the table. *Nobody will find me here!* he thought.

But Brian was wrong.
A little alien saw a lion's tail poking
out from under the tea table.
The alien grabbed a bowl of popcorn . . .

. . . and disappeared under the table too.

"**Zap-Zap! Gotcha!**" went the alien.
"I'm Caitlin. I come from the planet Zog."
Caitlin had springy, wobbly alien eyes.
They made Brian laugh.

"I'm Brian, and I'm a lion. I'm hiding
from the ballerinas and fairies!" he said.
"I'm hiding from the monster-mums," said Caitlin,
"I'll roar at any monster that comes near," Brian said.
"ROAR!"

"Wow, that's cool," said Caitlin.
She showed Brian her inter-galactic walky-talky.
"*That's* cool too!" said Brian.

Suddenly, Caitlin heard her name being called.

It was the magician.

"Ah! Here's the birthday girl!" he said, waving his wand and making his top hat spin round. He blew up a balloon that went **bang!** and turned into a lollipop.

"Right! I need a couple of helpers!" he said.
"Come on, Birthday Girl. And who
would you like to help you?"
"Brian the lion!" said Caitlin.

Brian and Caitlin held the magician's top hat.
He said some magic words and then out came a long woollen scarf,
a teddy bear, an umbrella, a watering can
and a . . . rabbit!
"Cool!" said the alien and the lion.

Next it was teatime, with pizza and chips
and lemonade and little cakes with
green icing and cherries on top.

And then . . . musical statues.
When the music stopped, Brian held his breath . . .
he didn't move . . .  he didn't even blink.
He almost won the prize . . .

. . . but he couldn't help laughing
at Caitlin's wobbly eyes!

The party was over much too quickly. Brian didn't want to leave.
"I helped an alien escape from the monsters," he told his mum.
"I called the spaceship through an inter-galactic walky-talky.
And I frightened the monsters with my mighty ROAR . . .
and . . . can we play again soon?"

His mum laughed.
"Of course you can!"
The lion swished his tail and the
alien jiggled her wobbly eyes.

"FIVE... FOUR... THREE... TWO... ONE... LIFT

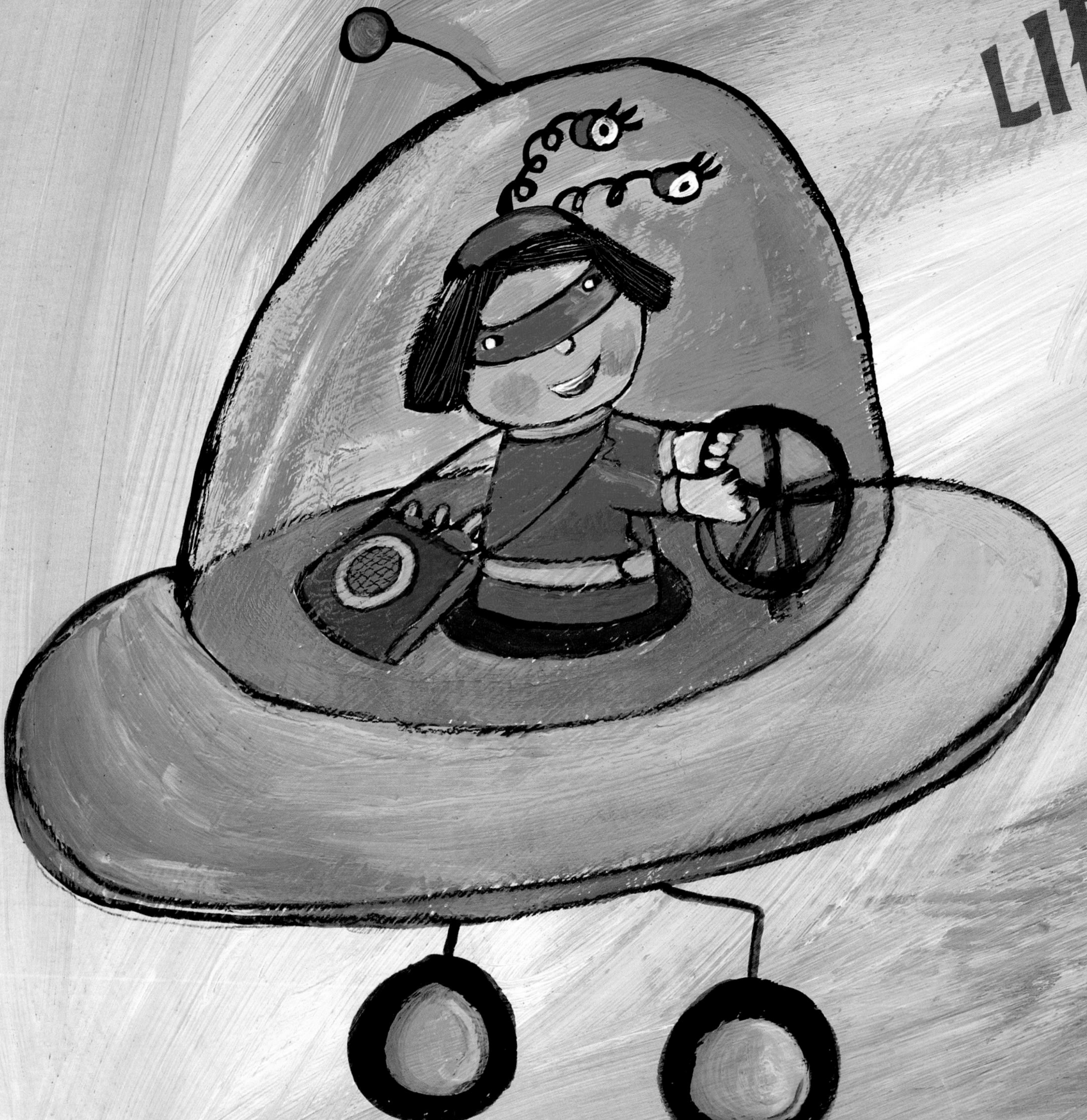

OFF!"

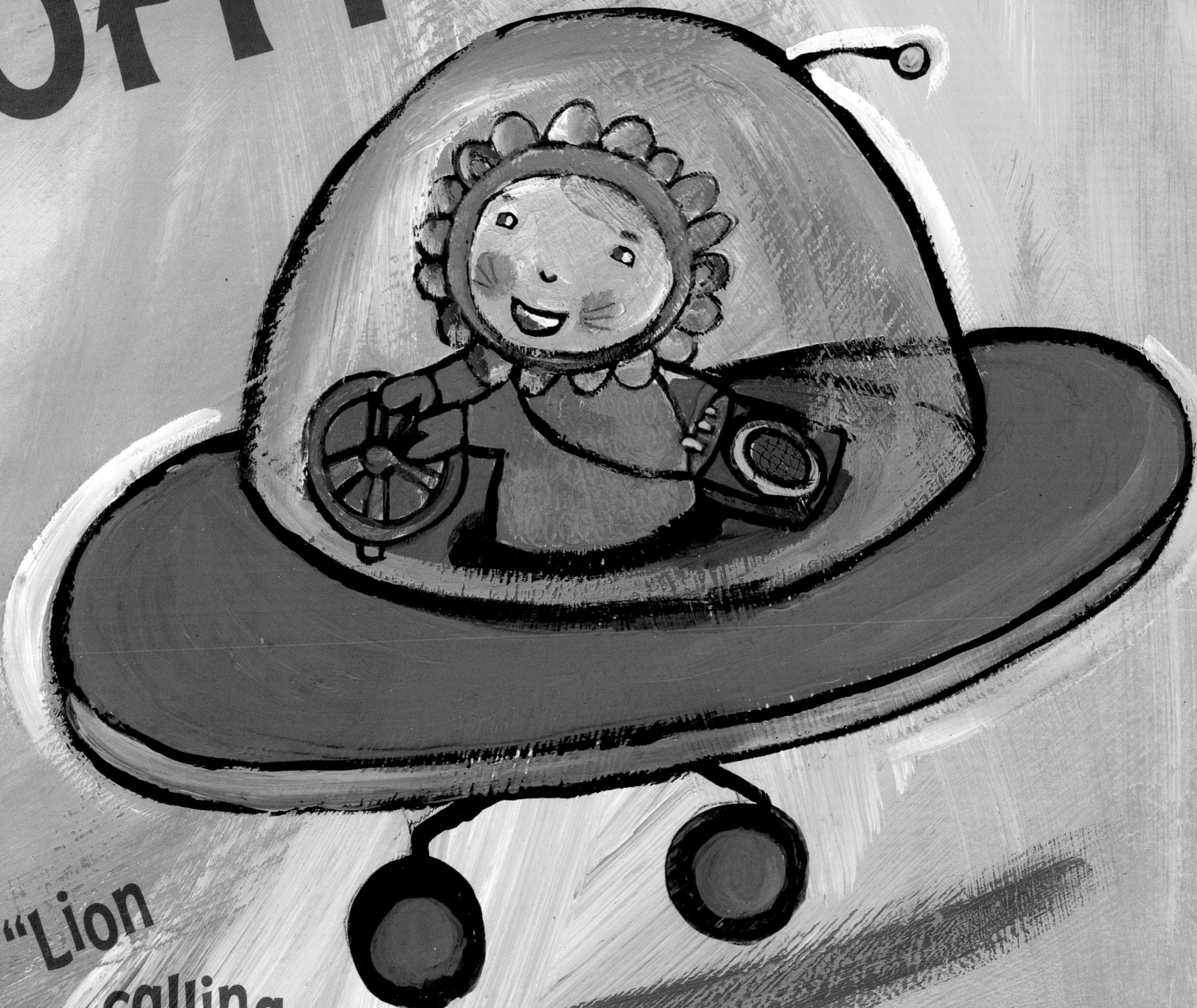

"Lion calling alien... monster alert, ggrrrrrrrrr!"

# Other Gullane Children's Books
## for you to enjoy

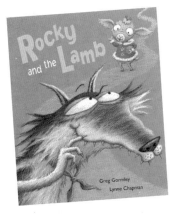

## Rocky and the Lamb
GREG GORMLEY •
LYNNE CHAPMAN

## Ten in the Bed
JANE CABRERA

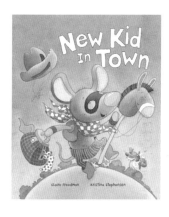

## New Kid In Town
CLAIRE FREEDMAN •
KRISTINA STEPHENSON

## Howling at the Moon
MICHAEL CATCHPOOL • JILL NEWTON